The
Easter Story

For Maureen Veronica

Great thanks to Mira Avrech, Abraham Rosenthal and the Israel Tourist Board
for their great kindness and generosity in the preparation of this book.

OXFORD
UNIVERSITY PRESS

Great Clarendon Street, Oxford OX2 6DP
Oxford University Press is a department of the University of Oxford.
It furthers the University's objective of excellence in research, scholarship,
and education by publishing worldwide. Oxford is a registered trade mark of
Oxford University Press in the UK and in certain other countries.

© Brian Wildsmith 1993

The moral rights of the author/illustrator have been asserted
Database right Oxford University Press (maker)

First published 1993
First published in paperback 1994
Reissued in paperback 1999, 2007
This new hardback edition first published in 2019

British Library Cataloguing in Publication Data
Data available

ISBN: 978-0-19-276873-5

1 3 5 7 9 10 8 6 4 2

Printed in China

Paper used in the production of this book is a natural,
recyclable product made from wood grown in sustainable forests.
The manufacturing process conforms to the environmental
regulations of the country of origin.

Brian Wildsmith
The
Easter Story

OXFORD
UNIVERSITY PRESS

Once, a long time ago, a little donkey was brought to Jesus.
The little donkey had never been ridden before, but Jesus spoke
gently to him, and soon he stopped being afraid.

Jesus climbed on to the donkey's back, and they set off for Jerusalem.

As they drew near to the city, there were great crowds
of people standing by the road. The little donkey was
amazed to see so many people.

Some had spread their clothes along the road. Branches cut down
from the palm trees were spread there too, all for him to walk on.
'Hosanna!' the people shouted.
'Hosanna! It's the man who comes from God.'

By the time they reached Jerusalem,
the crowds were filled with excitement.
Some people were asking, 'Who's that
sitting on the back of the donkey?'
Others replied, 'It is the prophet Jesus,
from Nazareth in Galilee.'

The little donkey lifted his head proudly
as they entered the city.

The little donkey carried Jesus through the streets
until they stopped in front of the temple. Jesus went inside
and saw that it was full of people busy buying and selling.

He drove them all out, shouting,
'My house is supposed to be a house
of prayer, not a den of thieves!'

For the rest of that week, the donkey stayed with Jesus in the city.
On Thursday night they walked through the streets to a small house,
and Jesus went in to have supper with his friends. Through the window
the little donkey saw Jesus breaking the bread.

'Take and eat this,' said Jesus. 'It is my body.'
And the donkey watched as Jesus lifted up a cup of wine.
'Take and drink this,' Jesus said. 'It is my blood.'

After supper, the little donkey followed Jesus
and his friends to the garden of Gethsemane.
Jesus said to them, 'Sit here and keep watch while I pray.'
The donkey sat and waited, but everyone else fell asleep.

Suddenly a crowd of people came into the garden.
They were led by Judas, one of Jesus' friends,
and they seized Jesus and dragged him away.

At this, the rest of Jesus' friends left him and ran.
The little donkey and Simon Peter didn't run away,
but followed the crowd through the city.

At last they came to the house of Caiaphas, the High Priest.
The donkey heard Caiaphas ask Jesus, 'Are you the Son of God?'
'I am,' Jesus replied.

Then the High Priest said, 'You have heard these terrible words. What do you say?' 'He deserves to die,' they all cried. The crowd left Caiaphas' house, and took Jesus to Pilate, the Roman Governor.

The little donkey watched as Jesus stood in front
of Pilate and a huge crowd of people.
'Are you the King of the Jews?' asked Pilate.
'Those are your words,' said Jesus.
The priests then accused Jesus of many things.

'Have you no answer to make?' said Pilate.
But Jesus did not reply.
'What shall I do with him?' asked Pilate.
'Crucify him,' they all shouted.
'Take him and crucify him, then,' said Pilate.
'I wash my hands of him.'

So the soldiers took Jesus away.
They put a crown made of thorns
on his head, and made fun of him.
'Hail, King of the Jews,' they said.
They gave him a huge cross of wood
and forced him to carry it.

'If only I could help him,' thought
the donkey sadly.
But a man came out of the crowd
and helped Jesus to carry his cross.

The little donkey followed as they led Jesus to a hill outside the city.

There they crucified him between two thieves.

Late that night, a rich man named Joseph
asked Pilate for the body of Jesus.
He wrapped the body in a clean linen sheet,
but it was too heavy to carry.

Joseph placed the body of Jesus on the donkey's back, and the little donkey carried it to a new tomb which had been cut out of the rock. Joseph laid the body inside and rolled a huge stone in front of the entrance.

Early on Sunday, two of Jesus' friends came to the tomb. But when they got there, they found that the stone had been rolled away and the body of Jesus was gone.

The donkey saw two angels where Jesus' body had been. 'He is not here,' the angels said. 'He is alive again.'

The women left the tomb and the donkey followed until they came to a garden. A man was standing there. The women thought that he was the gardener, but the little donkey knew it was Jesus.

The women were frightened, but Jesus said to them, 'Don't be afraid.
Run and tell my friends to go up to Galilee, and they will see me there.'

Jesus' friends were so happy to see him again. He stayed with them for forty days, teaching them about the Kingdom of God. But Jesus knew that it was near the time for him to leave this earth.

As the sun rose one morning, he went up to his father in Heaven.

The next day, one of Jesus' friends took the little donkey
back to his home. And the little donkey stayed there
for the rest of his life, remembering the kind and good man
he had carried on his back to Jerusalem.